Stories for Boys

Stories for Boys

LITTLE TIGER PRESS

London

Contents

I'm Not Going Out There!

Paul Bright   Ben Cort

I'm underneath the bed,
Hardly poking out my head.
It's a squeeze and hurts my knees,
but I don't care.
Can you guess, do you know,
Why I whisper soft and low?

I'M
NOT
GOING
OUT
THERE!

There's a dragon breathing smoke,
Who looks far too fierce to stroke,
And his eyes have got a scary sort of stare.
I hope he doesn't stay,
But he's not what makes me say,

I'M NOT GOING OUT THERE!

There's a ghost who's got no head,
With some toast and chocolate spread,
Which I'm sure he would be very
pleased to share.
And though I'd like a bite,
Still I'm keeping out of sight.

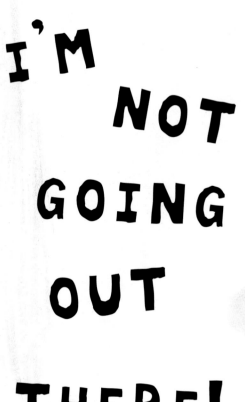

I'M NOT GOING OUT THERE!

There are witches, old and stubbly,
Round a bath all hot and bubbly,
Busy washing all their dirty underwear,
Hanging knickers out to dry,
But they're not the reason why

I'M NOT GOING OUT THERE!

There are monsters of all sizes,
Doing ballet exercises,
Wearing tutus, with pink ribbons in their hair.
And though they look quite charming,
There is something else alarming.

I'M NOT GOING

OUT THERE!

Then there's suddenly a shrieking
And a squealing and a squeaking,
Loud enough to give the boldest beast
a scare.
Now I'm shaking and I'm quaking,
There's a noise of something breaking.

I'M NOT GOING OUT THERE!

The dragon turns quite pale,
From his nostrils to his tail,
Feels a trembling in his tum:
"Oh, I really want my mum!"
"Mustn't panic!" gasps the ghost.
"Keep your head! Don't lose your toast!
I can haunt some other day,
Now I need to get away!"

The witches spill their washing
And go splishing, splashing, sploshing,
Soaked and soapy, slipping, sliding,
Searching for a place to hide in.
Hide from what? They'll soon find out!
They can hear it scream and shout,
And it doesn't sound like fun.
Better hurry! Better run!

23

The monsters don't feel brave,
But they know how to behave,
So they dance off in a row,
Each one on his tippy-toe.

Then all that I can hear,
Very loud and very near,
Is the thing that made them flee.
Do you know what it could be?

It's got teeth that can gnash,
It's got eyes that can flash,
I can hear it grumping, jumping,
Hear it stamping, stomping, thumping.
It's got hands that can snatch,
It's got nails that can scratch.
And it's ready for a fight,
So we're squeezed and
squashed up tight!

There it is – my sister Kate!
And she's in a frightful state,
Making shrieking sounds
and leaping in the air.
By now she must know who
Put the spider in her shoe . . .

... I'M NOT GOING OUT THERE!

In a factory, on a hill,
a huge machine made
robot dogs.

The robot dogs rolled out of the factory and were delivered to owners who played with them and loved them and cared for them.

The dogs were very happy because all dogs, even robot dogs, want an owner.

One little dog on the
conveyor belt was very
excited.

"I wonder what my
owner will be like,"
he said. "What will
I be called?"

He was much too
excited to sit still – he
jumped and frolicked and
bounced up and down. But then,

CRASH!

he bounced too high and clonked
his ear. At once alarm bells rang, red lights
flashed and a cloud of smoke whooshed as
the huge machine ground slowly to a stop.

The machine inspected the robot
dog very carefully. Finally
a voice boomed:

"NOT RUSTY OR DUSTY,

NOT BATTERED OR BENT,

NO PATCHES OR SCRATCHES,

BUT THERE IS A DENT!

SCRAP!"

"So that's my name!"
thought Scrap as the
machine picked him
up and dropped him
through a hatch.

44

Scrap slid down a shoot
and landed in a yard full of junk.
  There, staring at him, were
some other dogs.
  "Hello!" he said. "I'm Scrap!
Where am I? Where's my owner?"
  One of the dogs said, "You don't have
an owner – you're a reject like us."

Bumper, Dent, Scratch and Sniffer
all lived in the yard. They made
it comfortable and it was
a wonderful place to play,
just a bit messy, the
way dogs like it.

They often played with other
dogs who had owners.
But sooner or later their
owners would call:
"Come on, Shiny,"
"Dinner time, Sparkle."

Then they stopped
whatever they were
doing and ran home.

Seeing the other dogs
go off happily to their
owners made the yard
dogs feel a bit sad.

"Why don't we get an owner?"
said Scrap one day.

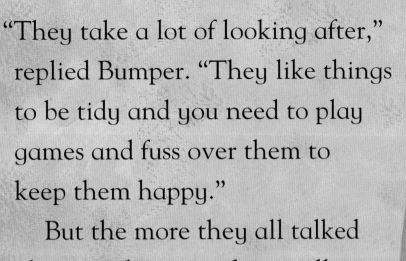

"They take a lot of looking after," replied Bumper. "They like things to be tidy and you need to play games and fuss over them to keep them happy."

But the more they all talked about it, the more they really wanted an owner.

"How can we get one?" said Sniffer. "We're rejects!"

"There must be a way," thought Scrap.

As Scrap started thinking, the cogs in his brain started turning. They went round faster and faster as he thought harder and harder.

Finally a light flickered on!

"I've got an idea!" Scrap announced to the other dogs, excitedly. "Come and help me!"

The dogs raced round collecting anything that might be useful.

They worked all day and all night and by the next morning the dogs were exhausted, but very proud, because . . .

. . . there stood an owner!

He was rusty and dusty, battered and bent, patched, scratched and covered in dents – but he had a heart of gold.

Their owner played with them and loved them and cared for them. And the dogs were very happy, because all dogs, even robot dogs, want an owner.

#0000

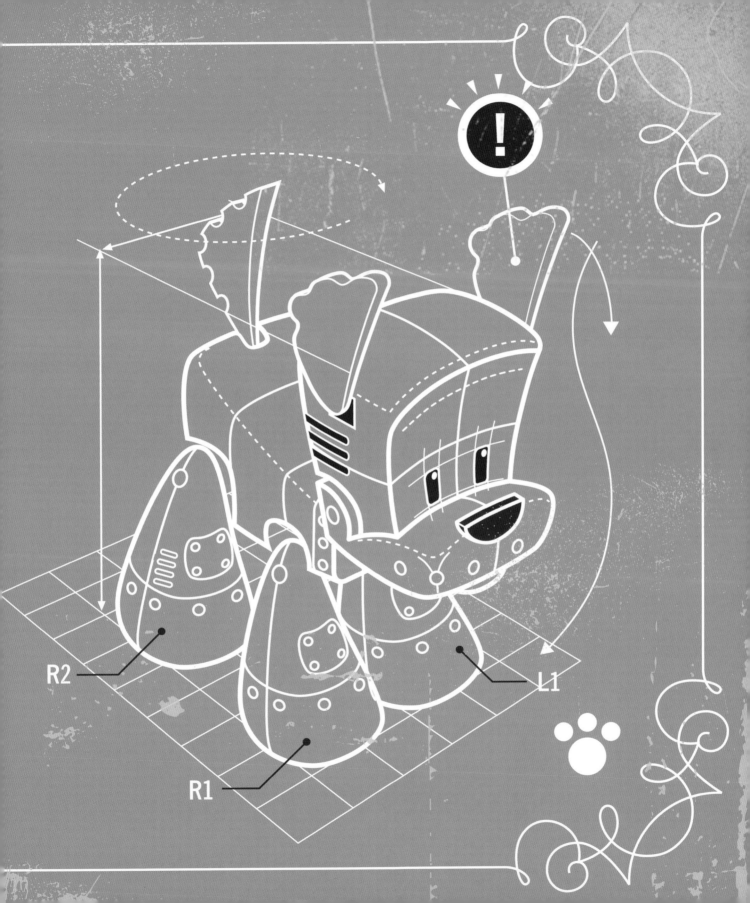

Don't Say That, Willy Nilly!

by Anna Powell

Illustrated by
David Roberts

"Willy Nilly," said his mother,
"would you like to go to the shop
and buy some cabbage for dinner?"
"YUK!" said Willy Nilly.

"Don't say that, Willy Nilly," said his mother. "Say, '**YUM, YUM, WHAT A LOVELY DINNER!**'"
"Yum, yum, what a lovely dinner?" repeated Willy Nilly.
"That's right," said his mother.
"**GOT IT!**" said Willy Nilly.
So Willy Nilly set off to the shop.

"YUM, YUM, **WHAT A LOVELY DINNER!**
YUM, YUM, **WHAT A LOVELY DINNER!**"
repeated Willy Nilly.

Outside the men were emptying dustbins.
Willy Nilly said, "Yum, yum,
what a lovely dinner!"

"Don't say that, Willy Nilly," said the dustbin men. "Say, **'GOOD RIDDANCE TO BAD RUBBISH!'**" "Good riddance to bad rubbish?" said Willy Nilly. "That's right," said the men. "**GOT IT!**" said Willy Nilly.

"GOOD RIDDANCE TO BAD RUBBISH! GOOD RIDDANCE TO BAD RUBBISH!"

In the road there was a big removal van.

The neighbours were moving away.

Willy Nilly said, "Good riddance to bad rubbish!"

68

"Don't say that, Willy Nilly," said Mrs Jiggs. "Say, **'ENJOY YOUR NEW HOME!'**"

"Enjoy your new home?" said Willy Nilly.

"That's right," said Mrs Jiggs.

"GOT IT!" said Willy Nilly.

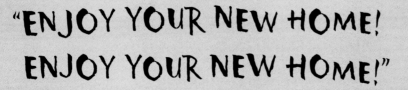

**"ENJOY YOUR NEW HOME!
ENJOY YOUR NEW HOME!"**
said Willy Nilly as he crossed the park.

The park-keeper was hooking some litter
out of the pond. He began to wobble and . . .

. . . fell into the water with a big

SPLASH!

"Enjoy your new home," said Willy Nilly.

"Don't say that, Willy Nilly," said the park-keeper. "Say, 'CAN I HELP YOU OUT OF THERE?'"

"Can I help you out of there?" said Willy Nilly.

"That's right," said the park-keeper.

"GOT IT!" said Willy Nilly.

"CAN I HELP YOU OUT OF THERE?
CAN I HELP YOU OUT OF THERE?"

Mr Totty's window was open. The parrot
looked at Willy Nilly with a beady yellow eye.
"Can I help you out of there?" said Willy Nilly.
"WATCH OUT, I MIGHT BITE!" said the parrot.

"Watch out, I might bite!"
said Willy Nilly.
"WATCH OUT, I MIGHT BITE!"
said the parrot.
"GOT IT!" said Willy Nilly.

"WATCH OUT, I MIGHT BITE!
WATCH OUT, I MIGHT BITE!"

On the pavement Willy met Granny Macaroon.

"Good morning, Willy Nilly!" said Granny Macaroon.

"Watch out, I might bite!" said Willy Nilly.

"Don't say that, Willy Nilly,"
said Granny Macaroon. "Say,
'**WHAT A LOVELY DAY!**'"
"What a lovely day?"
said Willy Nilly.
"That's right," said
Granny Macaroon.
"**GOT IT!**" said Willy Nilly.

77

"WHAT A LOVELY DAY!
WHAT A LOVELY DAY!"

The window cleaner sped past on his bicycle.

He wasn't looking where he was going.

He was heading straight for the lamp post.

"What a lovely day!" said Willy Nilly.

CRASH!

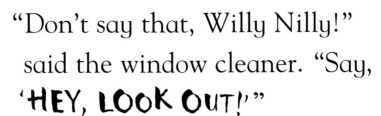

"Don't say that, Willy Nilly!"
said the window cleaner. "Say,
'**HEY, LOOK OUT!**'"
"Hey, look out!" repeated Willy Nilly.
"That's right," said the window cleaner.
"**GOT IT!**" said Willy Nilly.

In the shop, there was a baby in
a pram. Willy Nilly saw the baby
reach out to a tower of cans. Oh no!
The cans would fall on top of him.
"**HEY, LOOK OUT!**"
shouted Willy Nilly.

And the baby stopped! Just in time.
"Quick thinking, young man,"
said the shopkeeper. "What can I
do for you?"

"A cabbage, please," said Willy Nilly.
"And what would you like as a
thank you?" said the shopkeeper.
Willy Nilly chose his favourite
thing – ketchup. "Thank you very
much," he said.

Willy Nilly went straight home.

"Did you get the cabbage, Willy Nilly?" asked his mother.

"GOT IT!" said Willy Nilly.

"Thank you very much," said his mother, and she cooked the cabbage.

Willy Nilly poured ketchup all over his cabbage to make it taste nice.

"YUM, YUM, WHAT A LOVELY DINNER!"

said Willy Nilly.

"YUK!" said his mother.

THE END

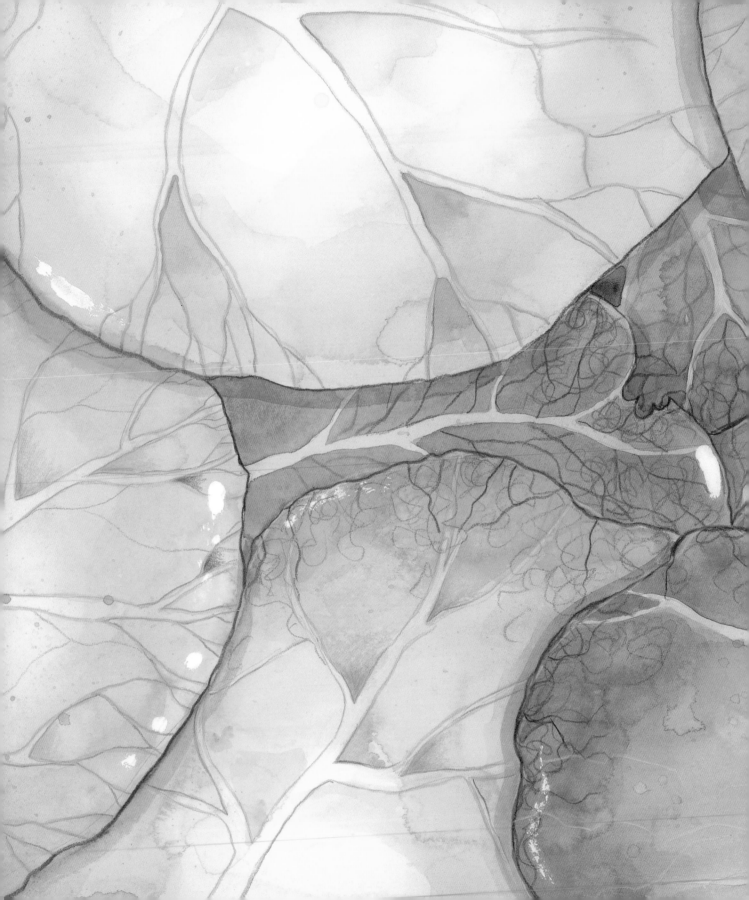

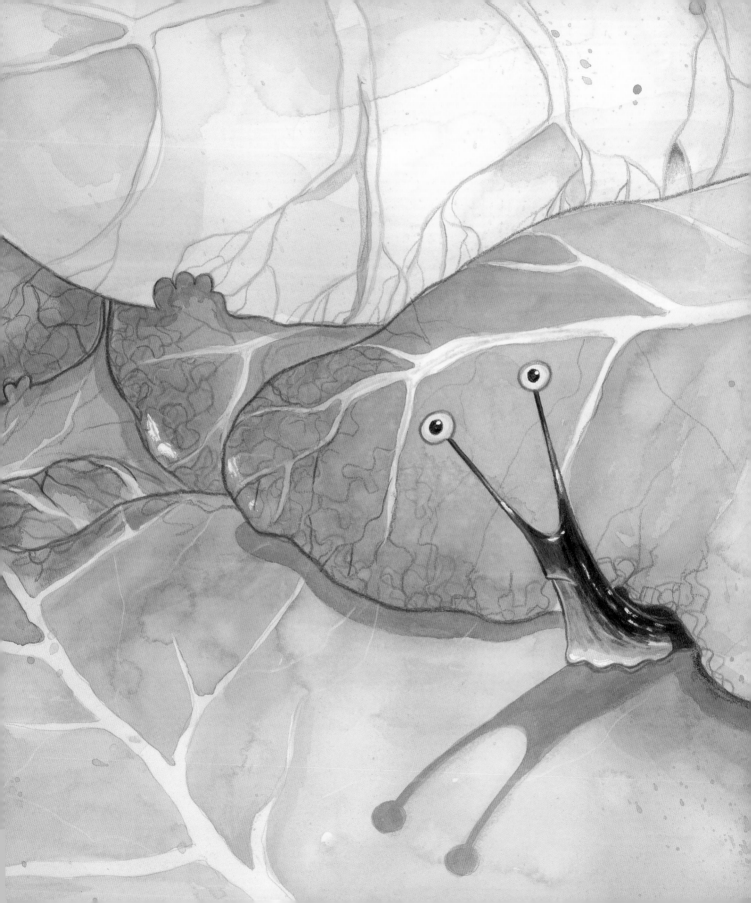

The BIGGEST, BADDEST WOLF

by
Nick Ward

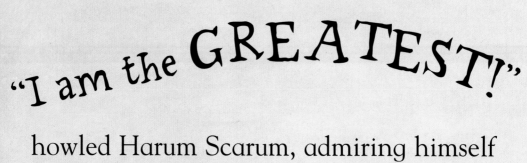

"I am the GREATEST!"

howled Harum Scarum, admiring himself
in the mirror as he brushed his fangs.
"I am the biggest, baddest, hairiest,
scariest wolf in the city!"

FUR
GEL

SHAMPOO
for extra
coarse hair

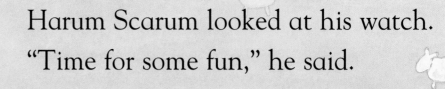

Harum Scarum looked at his watch. "Time for some fun," he said.

Harum Scarum's idea of fun was to scare people. Well, he was the biggest, baddest, hairiest, scariest wolf in the city!

"Have I got everything?" he wondered, patting his pockets. "Money, sweets, Teddy . . . Oops, where's my teddy?"

Nobody knew that Harum Scarum had a teddy, and that he couldn't go anywhere without him.

"Ah! There you are!"
he sighed, giving Teddy
a big, wet, wolfy kiss.

He put Teddy in his
back pocket and went
off happily.

First stop was the park where Harum Scarum
had some fun scaring all the little children
playing on the swings.

"Run, little children, run, or I'll **eat you up!**"

he howled.

"**Eeek!**" they screamed and rushed away.

"I am the biggest, baddest, hairiest, scariest wolf in the city!" he called after them.

Harum Scarum moved on to the bus stop,
where a group of old people were waiting.

"Run, old people, run,
or I'll eat you up!"

he howled.

"Eeek!" they screamed,
and tottered all the way home.

"I am the biggest, baddest, hairiest,
scariest wolf in the city!" he called
after them.

For the rest of the day
Harum Scarum worked
very hard at scaring
anyone he could. He
startled a skateboarder . . .

He petrified a builder . . .

And he made a street
juggler jump.

"This is fantastic fun,"
he cried.

By the time he got home, he was so tired
he decided to go straight to bed. And that's
when he discovered . . . he'd lost his teddy!

"Oh no!" he said, frantically searching
his room. He looked here and there . . .
but he couldn't find Teddy anywhere.

Harum Scarum crawled sadly into bed.
He tossed and turned, but he couldn't
get to sleep without his teddy to cuddle.

The next morning Harum Scarum was a nervous wreck. "I must find my teddy," he wailed, and hurried outside without even brushing his fangs.

He paced the streets. He searched in every alleyway. He looked high . . .

and low . . .

But Teddy was nowhere to be seen.

Finally he arrived at the bus stop.
  "Excuse me, have you seen a teddy?"
he asked the old people.

But as soon as they saw him they tottered off home shouting, "Help, it's the biggest, baddest, hairiest, scariest wolf in the city!"

Harum Scarum went to the park. "Excuse me . . ."
he began, but the little children all rushed off
shouting, "Help, it's the biggest, baddest, hairiest,
scariest wolf in the city!"

Harum Scarum sighed, and a tear rolled down his cheek. But just then he noticed one little boy left playing on his own. And he was playing with . . . Harum Scarum's teddy!

"My teddy!" gasped Harum Scarum.
"MY teddy!" said the little boy.
"Finders keepers."

"Please give him back,"
Harum Scarum whimpered.
"I'm the biggest, baddest,
hairiest, scariest wolf
in the city."

"You don't look so scary to me," said the little boy.

"Please!" cried Harum Scarum. "I'd do anything to get Teddy back."

"Do you promise to do exactly what you're told from now on?" smiled the little boy.

"Of course," he said.

The very next morning, after a good night's sleep, Harum Scarum brushed his fangs and patted his pockets. Whistling happily, he left home and went straight to the park.

"Hurry up," cried the little children. "We're on the swings! Come and push us."

"Coming," smiled Harum Scarum. He trotted up to the children . . .

"Run, little children, run, or I'll eat you up!"

"Eeek!" cried the children, rushing off. "You promised . . ."

"Well, what did you expect?" chuckled
Harum Scarum, hugging his teddy.
"You should NEVER trust the biggest,
baddest, hairiest, scariest wolf in
the city!"

Bored Bill

by Liz Pichon

Bill was bored. He wasn't just a little
bit bored, he was REALLY, REALLY bored.

Bill's owner Mrs Pickle was never bored.
She liked to keep busy ALL day.

Mrs Pickle loved reading,
but Bill thought reading
was boring.

Mrs Pickle adored gardening.
Bill thought gardening was
very dull indeed.

Mrs Pickle was a fantastic cook and a kung fu expert.
"Try this, Bill, it's fun!!" she said happily.
"Oh no," sighed Bill.

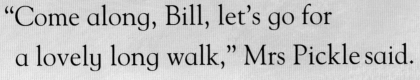

"Come along, Bill, let's go for
a lovely long walk," Mrs Pickle said.
"Borrrrrring," muttered Bill.
"Boring dogs get bored," said Mrs Pickle.
"Besides, it's no fun sitting around all
day doing nothing."
"I won't go," said Bill firmly.

Outside the weather was dreadful.
It was cold and windy. It was so
windy that Mrs Pickle's hat flew off.
"Whoooops!" Mrs Pickle laughed.
"How borrring," groaned Bill.

Suddenly a huge gust of wind
swept down and lifted them both
off their feet.
"YIPPEEEE!" squealed
Mrs Pickle as she disappeared from
sight. Bill clung to a tree when
SNAP! the branch broke
and he was spun up into the air.

Higher and higher he went. Faster and faster, past the moon and stars and up into space he flew.

"AT LAST!" cheered Bill.
"No more boring walks for me.
Space will be REALLY exciting."

THUMP!

Bill landed
on a strange
purple planet.

The noise woke up the aliens. They all popped up to see what it was. Bill was delighted to meet them.

"This planet looks like fun," he smiled. "I bet Mrs Pickle isn't having an adventure like this!"

Meanwhile, back on EARTH, Mrs Pickle gets rescued . . .

Bill asked the aliens to show him the whole planet.
"LET'S EXPLORE AND HAVE FUN!" Bill shouted.
"What's the point of exploring?" the aliens sighed.
"Exploring is borrrring."
"I'm hungry," one alien mumbled. So they all
went to have some squidgy green food.

"Fantastic!" thought Bill. "Alien food MUST be delicious."

But it wasn't. The squidgy green food was REVOLTING! Worse still, the aliens ate it for every single meal.

Life on the planet with the aliens was not very interesting at all. They just sat around all day long doing absolutely

NOTHING.

Bill had never been so bored.
He really missed Mrs Pickle
and her delicious food.

Bill looked at the aliens lying around the planet.
"Mrs Pickle was right!" he thought suddenly.
"Doing nothing all day is REALLY BORING!
We need to get BUSY."

"Come along!" Bill shouted to the aliens. "Boring aliens get bored. It's time to have some fun!"

Bill cooked the aliens a lovely meal, just like Mrs Pickle's.

He showed them some of Mrs Pickle's top kung fu moves.

Then they played some games, which everyone enjoyed.

NOBODY was bored any more.
But Bill still missed Mrs Pickle.
He wanted to go home.

So the aliens brought out their spaceship and flew Bill back down to earth. They all waved and said goodbye.

When Bill landed he found he was FAMOUS!

EVERYONE wanted to talk to Bill about the aliens. But the only person Bill wanted to see was . . .

...MRS PICKLE!

"I'll never be bored again!" said
Bill as he hugged Mrs Pickle.

So from that day on, Bill always kept himself busy, just like Mrs Pickle did. He read books and practised kung fu.

He dug the garden and cooked delicious food.

Bill even enjoyed doing the cleaning, which Mrs Pickle thought was very helpful . . .

. . . especially when they
had so many new
friends round for tea!

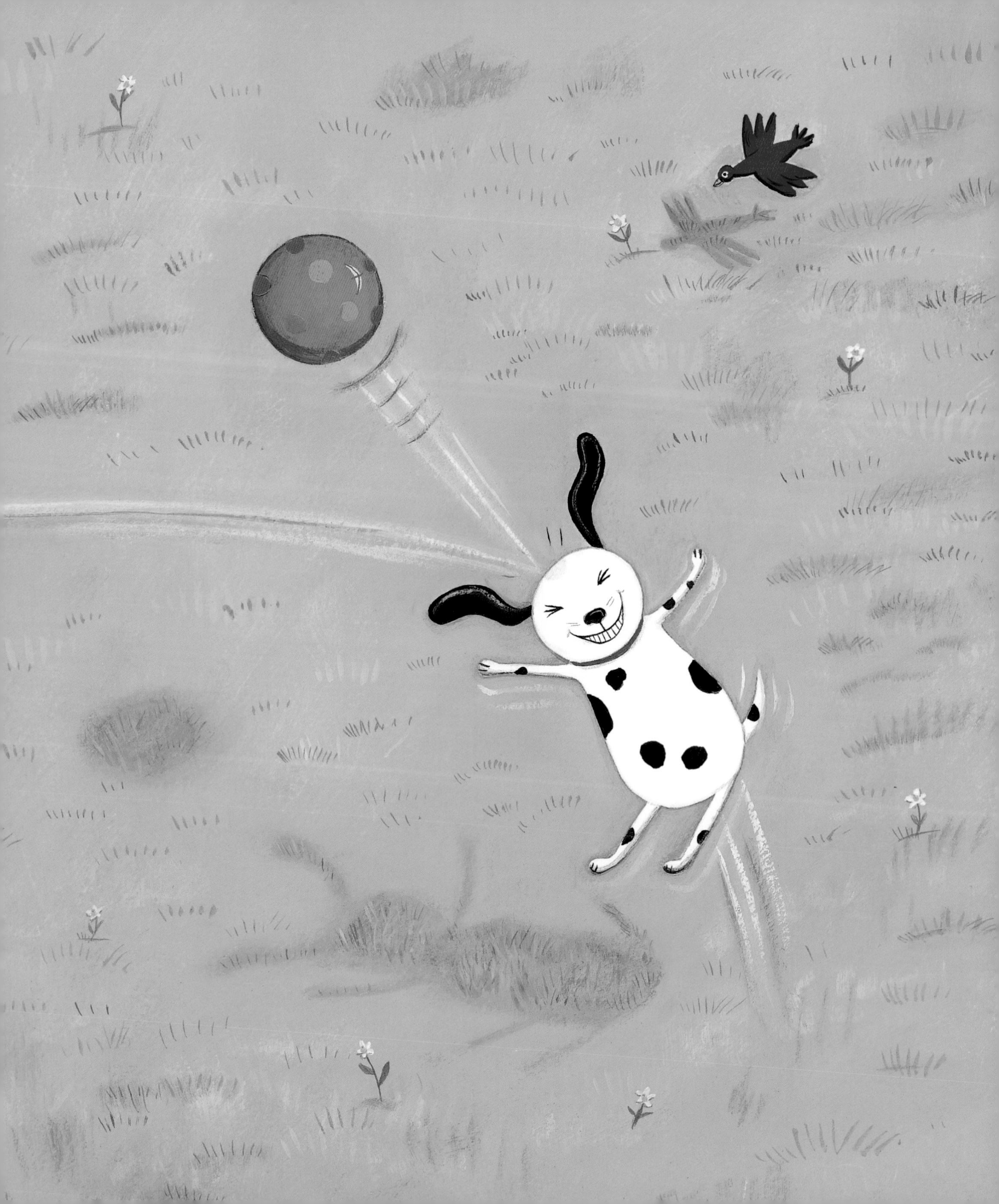

I'm Special, I'm Me!

Ann Meek   Sarah Massini

Milo looked in the mirror and sighed
a big sigh.

"Come on, Milo, we're going to be
late!" called Mum up the stairs.
Milo pressed his nose right up against
the cool glass.

"What am I going to be today?"
he whispered to himself.

147

At school Milo and his friends were playing a jungle game.

"Please can I be the lion?" asked Milo.

"No," said Clare. "You're not strong enough to be king of the jungle."

So Milo was a rather sad monkey.

When he got home Milo peered into the mirror.

"Who can you see?" asked Mum.

"A monkey," replied Milo quietly.

"Lucky you," said Mum. "How fantastic to be able to swing through the trees with all your monkey friends."

"Oh yeah!" said Milo, grinning and making monkey faces at his mum.

The next day the children were playing pirates.

"Please can I be the captain?" asked Milo.

"No," said Ben. "You're too short. The captain has to be tall."

So Milo had to be a deck hand.

"What's wrong?" asked Mum that evening.

"I wish I was tall, like a pirate captain," said Milo.

"I think you are just perfect," said Mum. "Just right for climbing to the top of the sails to be the look-out."

"Wow!" said Milo, smiling. "I never thought of that."

The next day the children were playing princes and princesses.

"Please can I be a prince?" asked Milo.

"No," said Jason. "The prince is handsome like me."

So Milo was an unhappy knight.

Later that afternoon Milo gazed into the mirror.

"Hello there, Milo," said Mum. "Who can you see looking back at you?"

"I can see a knight," said Milo.

"Terrific!" said Mum. "All that shining armour and you must be brave because only the bravest men are chosen to be knights, you know."

"Really?" said Milo, a little surprised.

"Definitely," said Mum.

"Cool!" said Milo, pretending to fight a dragon.

The next day the children were playing spacemen and aliens.

"I'd like to be an astronaut," said Milo, excited.

"No!" said Eloise. "Astronauts can't wear glasses because their helmets wouldn't fit."

So Milo was a little green alien.

Back home Milo gazed at his reflection in the mirror.

"Do I look like an alien?" he asked.

"You look just like you," said Mum. "Two eyes, a nose and a mouth, but different from everyone else and that's what makes you special, that's what makes you my Milo." Mum put her arms around him. "And anyway, aliens are so lucky to be able to bounce around in space speaking a secret alien language."

"That's true," Milo smiled. "*Bling, bling, yook, yook,*" he said, bouncing around his bedroom, trying to catch his mum.

163

The next day the children
were playing under the sea.
  "I'm going to be a shark,"
said Alex.
  "I know what I'm going to be!"
said Milo. "I think I'd be a good stingray,
hiding in the sand and swimming out and
surprising people and making them JUMP!"
  The children all stared at Milo . . .

165

"Great idea," said Ben.
"Brilliant!" said Clare.
"Can I be one too?"
asked Alex.
Milo smiled from ear to
ear, and ALL the children
played stingrays under
the sea for the rest
of the day.

"That was a great game, Milo," said Ben. "Let's play it again tomorrow."

Milo smiled the shiniest smile he had ever smiled.

When he got home that day, Milo
looked carefully into his mirror to
see if he had changed in any way,
but of course he hadn't.

"Mum was right," he said, "I can be
whatever I want to be – I'm ME!"

And in the mirror Milo's reflection
looked back with a huge, shiny smile!

STORIES FOR BOYS

LITTLE TIGER PRESS
1 The Coda Centre
189 Munster Road, London SW6 6AW
www.littletiger.co.uk

First published in Great Britain 2014

Printed in China
LTP/1800/0980/0914
ISBN 978-1-84895-956-9
2 4 6 8 10 9 7 5 3 1

I'M NOT GOING OUT THERE!

Paul Bright
Illustrated by Ben Cort

First published in Great Britain 2006
by Little Tiger Press

Text copyright © Paul Bright 2006
Illustrations copyright © Ben Cort 2006

ROBOT DOG

Mark Oliver

First published in Great Britain 2005
by Little Tiger Press

Text and illustrations copyright © Mark Oliver 2005

DON'T SAY THAT, WILLY NILLY!

Anna Powell
Illustrated by David Roberts

First published in Great Britain 2005
by Little Tiger Press

Text copyright © Anna Powell 2005
Illustrations copyright © David Roberts 2005

THE BIGGEST BADDEST WOLF

Nick Ward

First published in Great Britain 2005
by Little Tiger Press

Text and illustrations copyright © Nick Ward 2005

BORED BILL

Liz Pichon

First published in Great Britain 2005
by Little Tiger Press

Text and illustrations copyright © Liz Pichon 2005

I'M SPECIAL, I'M ME!

Ann Meek
Illustrated by Sarah Massini

First published in Great Britain 2005
by Little Tiger Press

Text copyright © Ann Meek 2005
Illustrations copyright © Sarah Massini 2005